ROSE DOYLE

THE STORY OF JOE BROWN

Rose Doyle is a Dublin writer and journalist. She is the author of thirteen novels, two of them for younger children and one for teenagers. She has also written radio plays, short stories and more journalism than she cares to remember. When not writing, she enjoys the company of friends, goes to films, walks, talks and compulsively reads.

All royalties from the Irish sales of the Open Door series go to a charity of the author's choice. *The Story of Joe Brown* royalties go to Kedron, Counselling and Psychotherapy Centre, St. Mary's Road, Edenderry, Co. Offaly.

NEW ISLAN

THE STORY OF JOE BROWN
First published 2004
by New Island
2 Brookside
Dundrum Road
Dublin 14

www.newisland.ie

Copyright © 2004 Rose Doyle

The right of Rose Doyle to be identified as the author of this work has
been asserted by her in accordance with the Copyright, Designs and
Patents Act, 1988

A CIP catalogue record for this book is available from the British Library

ISBN 1 904301 45 2

New Island receives financial assistance from
The Arts Council (An Chomhairle Ealaíon), Dublin, Ireland.

Typeset by New Island
Printed in Great Britain by CPD (Wales) Ltd, Ebbw Vale.
Cover design by Artmark

1 3 5 4 2

Distributed By:
Grass Roots Press
Toll Free: 1-888-303-3213
Fax: (780) 413-6582
Web Site: www.literacyservices.com

Dear Reader,

On behalf of myself and the other contributing authors, I would like to welcome you to the fourth Open Door series. We hope that you enjoy the books and that reading becomes a lasting pleasure in your life.

Warmest wishes,

Patricia Scanlan.

Patricia Scanlan
Series Editor

THE OPEN DOOR SERIES IS DEVELOPED WITH THE ASSISTANCE OF THE CITY OF DUBLIN VOCATIONAL EDUCATION COMMITTEE.

Chapter 1

Joe Brown had been staying less than a month in the hostel when things began to go wrong. Small, but irritating, things.

The first thing was that some of his books went missing. Then four pairs of socks got lost in the wash. Then the cherry yoghurts he kept for breakfast disappeared – every one of them. He'd had five in a container in the fridge. Things went from bad to worse when a new resident arrived. He was an older man who drank and didn't wash. He was given the bunk-bed beside Joe's.

Long before any of this, the dank loneliness of the recreation-room had been getting him down. With its brown walls, green floor, ancient 21-inch TV and twelve creaking wooden chairs, the place oozed despair. In no time at all it had eliminated the charms of freedom.

The "friend" who'd recommended the place was probably still laughing at his joke. Joe Brown cursed him and began looking for a room to rent.

He knew it wouldn't be easy to find, given his limited finances. His neatly written ads on the notice-boards in the local Spar and barbers hadn't got a single response. That he didn't have a mobile phone and that the hostel's public phone was out of order didn't help matters.

He found a room, and had his first sighting of Julia Ryan, on a grey November morning just two weeks into his search. Julia was hard to miss. Under a red wool coat, flapping open in spite of the cold, she wore jeans and a white T-shirt. She had silver hoops in her ears.

He was waiting to pay for his paper in the Spar when she came in. She stood looking around, saw the manager and went straight up to him. Smiling, tossing her blonde hair, she spoke to the man briefly. When he nodded, clearly captivated, she went to the notice-board and pinned a small card there. Then she left.

Joe left the queue and watched through the window as she walked briskly down the street. He knew she hadn't even noticed him. He knew he would read her notice as soon as she was out of sight.

He'd been going to the Spar every morning because there, at least, he was treated like an ordinary person. The young people behind the counter saw only an anorak-wearing male customer with a beard and glasses.

It was easy to become a nobody, he'd discovered. Very easy. The trick was not to give anyone a reason to take a second look at him or to think about him. He followed the same ritual every morning. He paid for his paper with the exact amount of money. If he bought milk or bread, he handed over the exact number of coins for them too. This attention to detail meant he never held up the queue or attracted attention. He was just as careful in every other part of his life.

He'd been different before. He'd enjoyed a chat then. He'd liked getting to know new people. It went against the grain to be so careful, but it had to be done. This way he didn't have to explain himself and face frozen smiles or abuse when people found out who he was.

Being friendly, exposing himself to hurt, had, in any event, been his downfall.

Once, soon after he'd re-entered the world and before he'd learned to be quiet about what had happened, a woman had actually hit him. She'd swung with her open hand and left a red weal across his face. He'd grown the beard after that, as a sort of protection as well as a disguise.

He'd stopped using his real name too. Hearing his name was what had enraged the woman. After a lot of thought, he'd settled on Joe Brown. It was a plain name. It didn't attract attention.

His own name and face, both of them far too well known, he committed to the rubbish bin of history. James Mulberry, with his limp brown hair and round, eager-to-please face, belonged in the past.

He liked Joe Brown, the name *and* the person he'd created to go with it. He was growing to like him more every day.

That morning, when Julia Ryan disappeared from view, he walked casually to the notice-board and read the notice she'd pinned next to his. She'd been every bit as precise as he'd been himself. She wanted a lodger. She was offering a room for rent in her house. It had an *en suite* shower and could be seen at any time. The rent included use of the kitchen. The address was in Copper Avenue, just two streets away.

Chapter 2

The second time Joe saw Julia Ryan she was standing in the doorway of her house. She was still smiling but wore a blue-and-white striped plastic apron over her jeans instead of the red coat.

Close up, he saw that she was older than he'd at first thought. Older than he was himself, even. But she was lovely, really lovely. She had blue eyes and dark lashes and skin that was as flawless as pouring cream. Joe Brown was thirty-two years old the day he met Julia Ryan. Julia was ageless.

The house was large and modern

but trying to look old. It had pillars each side of the door and many windows with small panes of glass. To Joe Brown, it didn't seem the kind of house whose owner would have needed to rent out rooms.

But things were rarely as they seemed in life, as he'd discovered to his cost.

"Have you come about the room?" Julia, standing in the doorway, sounded worried. She was a little breathless. Joe nodded and she opened the door fully. "Come on in then," she said. "I've just finished giving it a bit of a clean. It hasn't been used in a while."

Joe followed her up the blue carpeted stairs, then across a paler blue carpeted landing. She talked all the time. Nervously, he thought.

"I wasn't expecting anyone to come so soon." She fiddled with her hair as she spoke. "I thought it would take a few days …" She opened one of the white-painted doors off the landing.

"I had a notice on the board in the Spar myself –" Joe began.

"I hoped the person who put that up would reply!" She interrupted him, beaming. "Do you work around here?" she said.

"In the library," Joe replied, then stopped. Best not to give too much information. Joe Brown was a quiet fellow.

"In the library …" she echoed as she pushed open the door. "That's nice."

The room was to the back of the house. It had more frills and flounces than Joe cared for. But it was bright and the bed looked comfortable. It was also clean. Everything the hostel was not, in fact.

"Will it do?" She sounded even

more worried. Joe nodded and her expression became one of relief. "I'll need a few days to sort things out," she said. "Could you ring on Friday?"

He rang on Friday and moved in on Saturday.

Late in the evening, after he'd unpacked and sorted his few belongings, he wandered down to the kitchen to make himself a nightcap. He didn't really want one, but he was hoping to meet Julia before going to bed. He met her daughter instead.

"I'm Angie." She half-turned from the fridge. "I suppose you're the lodger." She gave him a cursory look before turning away to click her long fingernails on the fridge door. "Mum never has anything interesting in here." She was sulky and tapped her foot impatiently. "Always the same old junk. Would you like a yoghurt?" She made another half-turn, trying to smile and failing miserably. Her eyes were unfriendly. She looked to Joe to be about eighteen.

He felt as if he'd been hit in the stomach with a wooden plank. He'd been a fool, again. He'd slipped back into James Mulberry behaviour. He'd arrived here in a haze of bright dreams and silly ideas about himself and Julia becoming friends. More than friends, perhaps, in time. But his landlady was married. She had a grown daughter whose father, Julia's husband, would no doubt arrive home any minute. If he wasn't already in the house. Joe Brown had been very, very stupid. A woman like Julia was bound to be married.

He'd been spending too much time alone, losing touch with reality. This was a wake-up call and he'd better pay heed. He would not be so stupid again. As Joe Brown, he would pay his rent, keep his nose clean and put nonsense about cosy friendships with his lovely landlady out of his head.

Angie sat at the table eating a yoghurt. She made a half-hearted effort to be pleasant. But it was clear she didn't like him moving into the house. As dark as her mother was fair, she was every bit as good looking, though in a different way. Where Julia was doll like and blue eyed, Angie was strong boned with large brown eyes. She lacked her mother's lightness of touch too. She probably took after her father in temperament as well as appearance.

"We won't see much of each other," she said. "I work at night. In a club."

"Sounds interesting," Joe said. Angie shrugged. When the kettle boiled, she raised her eyebrows at him but didn't move.

"I'll just make myself a cup of tea," Joe said and got himself a mug.

"Whatever." Angie shrugged and finished the yoghurt. "Mother says you're a librarian." She looked bored.

"Yes," Joe said.

He was the library handyman, in fact, and lucky to have any job. But Angie didn't look like a library user, so let her think what she liked. It wasn't as if he'd never been a librarian. In prison, when they'd discovered his liking for books, they'd put him in charge of the library. But there was no shortage of people who liked books outside of prison. And libraries preferred to employ people without criminal records. Keeping the windows and the gutters clean was his job these days.

"Do you like to read?" he asked Angie.

"Nope. It's a stupid, boring waste of time." She reached behind her and turned up the volume on a small white television sitting on the work top. "Reading's for nerds –" She stopped and shrugged. He finished the sentence for her.

"Like me?" he offered.

"If the cap fits." She shrugged again. "What good did reading ever do you?"

The way she looked at him said it all. Angie Ryan was seriously under-impressed by her mother's lodger. He could have told her that reading had got him out of prison ahead of time. Instead, he said, "Would you like me to make you a cup of tea too?" and reached for a second mug.

"All right," Angie said. Joe turned

the kettle back on. It was white with a gold handle. Everything in the kitchen was either white or gold. The floor tiles were white with grains of gold running through them. It all looked very expensive.

Julia came into the kitchen while the kettle was boiling up again. "I'm glad to see you're making yourself at home, Joe," she said, filling the room with her smiling good humour. "And so is Angie. Aren't you, my pet?"

"Absolutely," Angie said.

"Have breakfast with us in the morning," Julia invited. "There's no need to be shy or to stand on ceremony. It's nice for us to have a man about the house. Isn't it, Angie?"

"Wonderful," Angie said. "Just wonderful."

Chapter 3

Joe's days formed a pattern after that.

The dull November mornings dawned a lot brighter in his new room than they had in the hostel. He found it easier to get up and a lot easier to feel hopeful about life.

Every morning he had a breakfast of cereal and toast with the Ryans, mother and daughter. Julia usually had it on the table for him when he arrived down to the kitchen.

"I'm not much of a cook," she said the first morning, laughing. "If you want boiled eggs, I could just about do them. Anything else you'll have to do yourself." She was wrapped in a soft, white towelling housecoat, her face smooth and young looking.

"Toast and cereal are just grand," Joe said. A coffee on its own was what he was used to. It would have done, but he didn't tell her that. He liked her fussing about him.

The days in the library, fixing and cleaning, became almost pleasurable now he had the evenings in Copper Avenue to look forward to. It took only a week for him to begin thinking of the house as home.

Most evenings Julia was there when he arrived in. There would be pizzas or TV dinners in the oven and a bottle of wine open on the table.

"Please don't be embarrassed," she said the first evening. "I like company for my evening meal and Angie's never here. You'll be doing me a favour, eating with me."

So eating together became part of the pattern too. They talked a lot, about nothing much but easily. Julia never asked him about himself. He never brought up the subject of a Mr Ryan. If he was dead or gone, fine. Better still if he'd never existed.

But if he was alive and due home any day, Joe Brown didn't want to know. He was enjoying things too much the way they were. Time enough to face reality when the bubble burst. As he felt sure it would. For now, for these short November days, it was a case of seize the day – *carpe diem*, as an old lag who was a something of a Latin scholar used to say. Not that it had done *him* a lot of good. He was in prison because he'd seized the chance to rob his banker employer and been caught.

Joe had no idea why Julia Ryan didn't question him about his life. He was just glad. He didn't want to have to lie outright to her.

He took to helping her wash up after dinner. But he was careful not to push things too far. When everything was dried and put away, he would say a polite good-night and go to his room. He knew better than to outstay his welcome.

At the beginning of the second week, Julia asked him to watch television with her.

"I've a bit of reading to do for tomorrow," he lied. "But thank you."

"If you change your mind, I'll be here," Julia said lightly. "Me and the television."

She seemed a little hurt. But he still

thought it was better to keep his distance. He was afraid of them becoming too close too soon, so he stayed in his room most nights, looking at the TV there. Twice a week he went to the gym.

Julia rarely went out at night. When she did, she came home early. She liked the movies, she said, and an occasional drink with friends.

Angie seemed to stay in bed all day. Joe had no idea what kind of club she worked in. He didn't ask questions about that either. He didn't ask anything at all about Angie. If he took to asking questions, then Julia might too.

He did look, discreetly, for signs of a Mr Ryan. There were none: no clothes or personal belongings; nothing in the bathroom, kitchen or living-room to indicate that another man had a home there.

He listened too. But as far as he could make out there were never any loving phone calls. Joe Brown felt himself growing happy. It was a feeling he didn't trust.

"What will you do for Christmas?" Julia said to him at breakfast on the Monday of his third week in the house. It was early December. The usual seasonal hysteria was in the air. He'd liked the hysteria, and everything else that went with Christmas, once.

"I haven't made any plans yet," he said, carefully.

The truth was that he'd been more than a little put out by his mother's reaction when he'd phoned about going home for Christmas. The neighbours were still "hostile" to him, she said. Seeing him would rake up memories for them. It would make it harder to forget what had happened. People still talked about it. The newspapers hadn't forgotten either. Someone had been around the place, snooping, in recent months.

It would be better, his mother said, if he waited until after Christmas. Until the spring perhaps, when people were feeling a little more cheerful about life in general. "I have to live with them all the year round and you don't," she said. The way she said it, he knew his absence would be the best Christmas present he could give her. Joe had wished her a happy Christmas and said another goodbye to James Mulberry.

In the kitchen, he watched Julia carefully as he said, "I was half thinking I might take a trip somewhere for Christmas. I'm not a great person for celebrating and festivities." He didn't feel like being around when Mr Ryan arrived home for Christmas. He'd decided, anyway, that Joe Brown would not be a party animal. James Mulberry had loved a good time, never leaving a party until dawn crept into the sky.

"I like a quiet Christmas myself," Julia said, smiling. "It's a lonely time of year, don't you think?"

"It can be," Joe said.

"Angie and I would like you to spend Christmas with us," Julia went on. "That's if you don't go away, of course. We'll be alone, and you know what they say?" She shook her head and gave a rueful laugh. "Two is company and three is a crowd. A crowd would be nice this Christmas. There were just the two of us last year …" She was talking quickly now, too quickly. "I was planning on getting a turkey. I'll cook it myself. First time ever. I'll buy in everything else, including a big pudding. Just in case my cooking doesn't work out. We'll have stuffing and cranberry sauce and …"

Further ideas for the menu failed her. She stopped, holding her hands up in an attitude of surrender.

"What would you like for Christmas dinner, Joe?"

He found himself adding smoked salmon and Christmas crackers to the list. Before he left for work, he found too that he'd committed himself to spending Christmas with his landlady and her daughter.

Chapter 4

It was exactly a week later when the two men arrived at the house in Copper Avenue.

Joe was in bed reading when the doorbell rang. A day spent trying to keep the ancient heating system in the library alive had tired him out. The bell rang a second time before he heard the living-room door open and Julia cross the hall to answer it. It was a little after nine o'clock, a late enough hour for anyone to come visiting.

Joe's heart gave a quick, uncomfortable skip in his chest. There was always the chance that it might be someone looking for him, the vengeful arriving to get him. Some people, he knew, could never let the past just be.

He told himself he was a fool. But he turned off the light and got off the bed anyway. He opened his door, a little, just as Julia opened the hall door.

"Thought we'd make a seasonal call," a man's voice said. "See how you were keeping, Julia." His tone was deadpan. It was hard to tell if he was being friendly or ironic.

"You're looking well at any rate," a second man said and gave a small laugh. He sounded older than his companion. "But then you always did. Lovely Julia." He paused. When Julia said nothing, he snapped, "It's cold out here." The laughter was gone now. "Aren't you going to ask us inside?"

"I wasn't planning to, no." Julia's

voice was hard, but with an edge of what Joe recognised as fear in it too. "I'd prefer if you would just leave."

"Now, now, Julia." The second man spoke again, in a mocking voice. "No need to be like that. It's Christmas time, after all."

A small shuffling was followed by the sound of the door closing.

"It's a sad case when we have to invite ourselves inside the home of an old friend," the first man said. "I thought you'd make us more welcome than this, Julia."

"What is it you want?" Julia said. Her voice had risen.

The first man spoke again. "The place is looking very well. Very well indeed. Tell me, how's that beautiful daughter of yours? Is she doing well too?"

Joe risked opening the door another

half-inch. He could see the top of
Julia's head and, facing her, what he
took to be the younger man. He was
about Joe's age, tall and dark and with
a tautness about him that told Joe he
was fit and strong. He was probably
used to handling himself in unwelcome
situations – or creating them. He wore
an ear-ring in one ear.

The other man, standing a little
apart and looking around the hall, was
about forty-five or fifty. He was fat
with lank hair in need of a wash. His
hands were stuffed into the pockets of
a heavy, navy wool coat.

"Come into the living-room," Julia
said stiffly. They followed her. Once
inside the room, the fat man closed the
door. Joe was left with nothing to tell
him what was going on but the muffled
sound of their voices.

They stayed about forty minutes.

Joe, at first, listened with his ear to the opening in the door. When this proved useless, he opened it wider and slipped silently into the shadows of the landing. He felt reasonably safe. He could always pretend he was crossing from the bathroom if anyone appeared. The men did most of the talking. Julia's voice interrupted now and again. But for the most part she was silent.

When one of the men raised his voice, Joe picked up a few words and phrases. "Long enough" was followed by "out of here" and, in a rush before the other man silenced him, "he's changed, but not that much. You'd better watch what you do, Julia."

They spoke in lower voices after that. Joe thought at one point that a fist banged a table. But he couldn't be sure. The end came with the sound of a chair being moved back and the voices coming closer to the door. Joe made it back to his room just before the men came out into the hall.

They left quickly, before he had a chance to have another look at them through the chink in his door. He swore as he shut it, hoping he'd timed it to close before Julia turned from the front door. She hadn't said good-night to the men. Their visit disturbed him more than a little. There had been too much that was familiar about them. A roughness. A bullying and threatening air. They were either policemen or criminals.

He couldn't be sure, but Joe thought Julia stopped outside his door on her way to bed that night. He gave a small cough, but she didn't knock or call his name as he'd half hoped she might. A moment later, he heard her bedroom door open, then close as she went inside.

That night, for the first time since moving in, he didn't sleep.

Chapter 5

"I hope my gentlemen callers didn't disturb you last night," Julia said at breakfast.

She was smiling as always, her head to one side and an eyebrow raised in query. As always in the morning too, she was all in white, even to the fluffy mules on her feet. Smiling back at her, unable to resist, Joe for the first time saw a shadow in her eyes.

"Not at all," he lied. She looked at him for a moment before reaching for the jug.

"I'm glad of that," she said. "Because

I would have preferred it myself if they'd stayed away." She poured milk over the cornflakes in her bowl. "They weren't welcome. I hope they never come again."

Stirring the milk into the cornflakes, she wasn't smiling any longer. Her bottom lip trembled and she swallowed, hard. With an obvious effort of will, she looked up again at Joe, trying to smile.

"Forgive me," she said. "I shouldn't involve you in my troubles. Please forget I said anything. And please be assured, too, that there's no reason for you to worry. That pair will never bother you. It's not their style to take on someone their own size."

She lifted a small helping of cereal on the spoon and sat looking at it without bringing it to her mouth. Joe, staring at her, was horrified to see a tear fall, then another. She sat silently as her eyes reddened and the tears rolled in a slow river down her face.

He sat, unmoving, utterly unable to decide what he should do. No point offering her a napkin, as she had one of her own. If he reached to touch her hand, clenched and small on the tablecloth, he might frighten her. Leaving his chair to go and put an arm about her might be worse. It might bring on hysterics or outrage. You never knew with women. That was his experience, anyway.

There was a clatter as she dropped the spoon of cereal and buried her face in her hands.

"I'm so sorry," she said, her voice muffled between her fingers. "So very, very sorry. I didn't want to involve you in any of the ugly things that have happened in my life. I thought it was all over, all the horror of the past gone and finished with forever. I thought we were safe at last, Angie and I."

She dropped her hands and looked at him, briefly, with eyes that were both angry and fearful. But still lovely.

"I had opened the door before I realised who they were" she said.

She was staring straight ahead now, sitting rigidly with her hands tightly clasped in front of her. "It was like a nightmare come to life, seeing those faces. I'd hoped never to see them again." She turned to look at Joe. "There was nothing for it but to let them come inside. I know them. They would have broken down the door if I hadn't."

"What sort of animals are they?" Joe found his voice at last. He found anger too. It liberated him, gave him the courage at last to reach out and touch her hands, so tightly knotted together. She didn't move them from under his.

"Who are they? Why are you so afraid of them?" he demanded.

"You don't need to know who they are, Joe," Julia said, her eyes on his. She shook her head with a slow sadness he couldn't bear. "A man like you shouldn't ever have to know men like them."

"You don't know what kind of man I am," Joe pointed out. "You only think you know me."

"You're a good man," Julia said. "I know that much, at least." She shook her head, sighing. "You're not the kind of man who would ever have dealings with men like the two who came here last night. I'm certain of that too."

She gave a small, brave smile. He felt a knot tighten in his heart. Just let those two boyos return. Just let them come back and frighten her again. If they did, and if they so much as touched a hair on her head or said a crooked word, they would have him to reckon with. And he was not a man to be lightly reckoned with. Others had found that to their cost. One man in particular.

"Don't answer the door if they come calling again," he said. "Come to my room and tell me. I'll answer the door. I'll deal with them."

"Oh, Joe." She moved her hand from under his and touched his face, very lightly. Then she blew her nose in the napkin. "You can't imagine what you would be letting yourself in for," she said. "They're dangerous people. They don't know what decency is, or how to behave around good and courteous people like you." She stood up. "I'll make the tea. You'll be late for your job if I don't. I don't want that on my conscience as well as everything else."

"The job will wait," Joe said, gruffly.

He watched the way she straightened her shoulders as she plugged in the kettle. He knew now that her smiling cheerfulness was a mask. It was a way of hiding her fear and dealing with some dark secret in her life. You just never knew with people. You could never tell what was really going on in their minds. Her thinking he was a good person was an example. It was a long time since anyone had made the mistake of thinking of him as a good person. He wanted to be a good person again, for her.

"I'll look after you," he said.

The words were out before he could stop them, filling the quiet of the kitchen and making her turn her head quickly.

"No, Joe," she said. "I can't have you

getting involved." But her eyes were full of hope.

"There's no good you saying 'no Joe' to me." He smiled. He hadn't felt so confident, so sure that he was doing the right thing, for a long time. "I'll be looking after myself too," he joked. "I can't have my landlady frightened out of her home. I'd have to leave then myself. And I've grown too fond of my little room for that."

He would have added that he'd grown fond of his landlady too, if he'd had the courage. But his bravery was of a different sort.

"They don't know about you living here." She kept her back to him while she carefully scalded the teapot and put in three tea-bags. Exactly as she did every morning. "They wouldn't have been so daring if they'd known there was a man in the house. It was easy to come here when they thought I was on my own."

"They didn't look all that fit and able to me," Joe said. "The shorter one could do with losing a couple of stone in weight." He smiled again, trying to reassure her.

"So you saw them, then?" Julia put the lid on the teapot and turned to look at him. "I thought so."

He said nothing as she poured the tea, first her own, because she liked it weak, then his. She put some milk in her cup and passed him the jug. Then she sat down and said, "Why did you hide in the shadows on the landing, Joe?" She looked at him over the rim of her cup as she sipped from her tea. Her voice was flat. Disappointed, he thought.

"I didn't want to be seen," he said, simply. She nodded and gave a small shrug. He decided the look on her face was one of resignation.

"I can understand that," she said. "But why did you lie to me? Why did you pretend to me that you hadn't seen them?"

"Because I was afraid it was me they'd come looking for," he said.

"Why would you think that? And why would you be afraid?"

"Because I'm not what you think I am –"

"And what do I think you are, Joe?" she interrupted gently.

He thought for a minute. She let him be, sipping her tea quietly and waiting for him to answer. He came to a decision and said, "I'm not a librarian."

"I know that."

"I'm a maintenance man at the library." He heard the desperation in his voice.

"I know that too." She looked at him. She went on looking at him, even when he dropped his eyes and fiddled with his cup. He could feel her eyes on him, direct and blue and questioning. He turned the cup round and round in its saucer. She was the only person he knew who didn't use mugs for tea.

He came to another decision.

Chapter 6

Joe Brown looked Julia in the eye as he began his story.

"I'm lucky to have got *any* job in the library," he said. "I've been out of work for a long time. I didn't have much by way of references." He paused, then went on quickly. "I was away for five years. I got a bit out of touch with things …" He stopped again. It was impossible to go on.

"Where were you?" Julia said, gently.

He couldn't tell her. It would change everything. She would ask him to leave.

He'd be back in a bunk-bed in the hostel, kept awake by the snores and drunken self-pity of the other losers. He was Joe Brown now. He wanted to remain Joe Brown.

The silence stretched. It felt as if the entire morning must have passed. Then Julia tapped her pink-enamelled nails briskly on the table. Her voice was brisk too when she said.

"Time to grow up, Joe. Time to face reality. I know who you are and what you are. I just thought it would be better for you to tell me yourself." She sighed and pulled a rueful face. "Did you really think I would take a lodger into my house without sussing him out? Let a man I didn't know share the house with my daughter and me without knowing all about him?"

"I suppose not …"

He'd been a fool. The same damn fool he'd always been. Worse, really, because he'd been given a chance to learn and hadn't taken it. He pushed back his chair and stood up.

"You'll want me to leave …"

"Sit down." Julia was impatient, tapping her fingernails on the table and glaring up at him. Joe sat back at the table. "I took a chance when I decided to have you here," Julia said. "I wasn't wrong then and I'm not making a mistake now either. Knowledge is power they say, and they're right. When I discovered your story, I decided that knowing about your past was all the protection I needed."

"How …?"

"I went to the library. They told me about you." She frowned. "I read your story in the newspaper files there. It seemed unfair. Five years for a pub brawl. I was struck by the unfairness of it."

"A man died," Joe said. "A man who'd been my friend and who was only twenty-four years old. He died because of me. Because I'd had too much to drink and lost control. It shouldn't have happened."

"You didn't set out to do it," Julia said. "That's the main thing. That was clear from the report of the court case too. That was what decided me in the end to let you stay living here." She gave a small smile. It had something of her old gaiety in it. "Tell me James Mulberry's story," she said.

He told her then how he'd gone drinking with a group of friends, young men he'd known all his life. They were all in their twenties then. It had been a night no different from many others: the same pubs, same talk of football, girls, music.

"It's hard to say, exactly, when the mood of the night changed," Joe said. "I remember closing-time being called in the pub. I remember us discussing which night-club we'd go on to. There were two girls with us, but I've no memory of how they came to join us. Sean Maguire had an arm about each of them."

He stopped. It was years since he'd spoken the name of the man he'd killed. He'd whispered it to himself many, many times but never said it aloud. Julia sat quietly while he took several deep breaths. After a while he went on.

"The argument about where to go was going nowhere, so the barman threw us out. There were still a few people in the street but no taxis about. None of us had a car. Anyway, we weren't fit to drive." He stopped again.

"What happened next is a blur. We were fighting, all of us, friend against friend. I still don't know why. Drink, I suppose. The demon drink –"

"The court report said you started it," Julia interrupted. "You attacked Sean Maguire."

"That's what people tell me." Joe put his head in his hands. "Maybe I did. But why? What led up to it?"

He took his hands away and looked at her. His eyes were steady now that he'd broken the barrier of not being able to talk about what had happened.

"I've no clear memory of anything after we came out of the pub. Nor of the last hour in the pub either, if I'm to be honest. They say I killed Sean Maguire. That I went after him like a madman and shoved him through the pub window. All of my friends and two other witnesses say they saw me do this. They must be right. I don't remember."

He took a gulp of his tea. It was cold. He added a spoon of sugar to give it some life. It still wasn't drinkable, so he pushed it aside. He could have done with a hot cup. But he thought it would be crass to leave the table to make one. Even worse to ask Julia to do it. Certainly not the kind of thing Joe Brown would do.

"I believed your version of things in the newspaper reports of the court case," Julia said. She was drinking her own tea, not seeming to notice how cold it was. "It seemed to me you were a young man made to take the blame for an accidental death. You're not a murderer, Joe. *I* don't believe you are, anyway."

He sat very still, unable to look at her for the tears in his eyes. No one had ever told him they didn't believe he was a murderer, not a single person since the night it all happened. Not even his mother. True, no one had actually called him a murderer either. Not exactly. They'd all just moved back, out of his life.

"Enough is enough," was all his brother had said by way of explanation. Nothing more.

"Thank you, Julia," Joe said when he felt able to trust his voice. "Thank you for that."

Then, because he felt they'd talked enough about him, and also because he really wanted to know, he said, "Tell me about the men who were here last night. Who were they? Why did they frighten you so much? Will they be back?"

Julia Ryan left the table with the teapot. She busied herself emptying tea-bags and waiting for the kettle to boil. Her shoulders were very straight; rigid, in fact. She seemed terribly fragile.

"They came on behalf of my husband." She spoke without turning around. "They're not friends of his exactly, more like accomplices. They say there's honour among thieves, don't they?" She turned. "Kettle's boiled. Would you like coffee this time, or will I make tea again?" She seemed distracted.

"Tea. Thank you. I have to say I didn't notice any honour among the thieves I met in prison. Just plenty of lying and treachery."

"I suppose you'd know." She turned to make the tea. "But it does seem to me that there's a sort of honour among George and his accomplices. They're all thieves, every last one of them. George is the biggest thief of all."

"George is your husband?" Joe asked.

She nodded and stood watching a cat cleaning itself on the wall behind the house. She had become very still again.

"Was he a thief when you married him?" Joe asked. He was becoming worried about her. She was too restrained by far. Another woman would have been angry, railing against a husband who had let her down and whose mates made threatening night-visits.

"He was always a thief, only I didn't know it when I married him." She spoke in a flat, thin voice. The cat moved off, eyeing a hungry bird. Julia brought the tea to the table and sat down. "We were married for two years when he was caught the first time. That was for a job on a jeweller's shop. Angie was six when he got out of jail. She was ten when he went to jail again, for house burglary. He tied up an old man that time, so he got another four years. We moved here when Angie was seventeen. I don't know where the money for the house came from and knew better than to ask. I live in fear of it being taken away from me."

She began pouring the tea: first her own, then Joe's.

"I told him if he ever went to jail again our marriage would be over. He was caught and put back inside just over a year ago. He got two years that time, but he's getting out early for good behaviour. He's had enough of jail."

She lit a cigarette. Joe had never seen her smoke before. But the box was open when she took it from her dressing-gown pocket, so it wasn't her first ever smoke.

"He'll be home for Christmas." She blew a smoke ring. "The messengers who came with the news last night were Leo Mahony and Charlie Owens. Faithful followers and dangerous when they have to be." She pulled on the cigarette until Joe thought her cheeks would cave in.

"They tell me he's coming here and that I have to take him in. They say it'll be bad for me if I don't. There's money he stole in this house, hidden upstairs. They say he wants to lie low here for a while, that he has plans to make. Then he'll take his money and be gone. That's what they say, anyway. But I don't want him staying here. He can take his money and go, now."

She wasn't rigid and controlled anymore. She was shaking from head to toe, her teeth chattering.

Chapter 7

Joe was out of the chair and kneeling with his arms about her before he could stop himself. Before she could stop him.

"You're not alone," he said. "And you don't have to be afraid. I'm here and I'm not leaving. Just tell him he can't stay. He'll be on probation. He won't want any trouble."

Julia leaned her head on his shoulder. He patted her hair, awkwardly, suddenly afraid of how close they were, of Angie appearing, of his own loneliness.

"You're on probation too." Her voice was low and hopeless sounding. "You don't want to get yourself into trouble either." She lifted her head. "You're a kind man, Joe Brown. I saw it in your face the day you arrived at my door." Her eyes were red from crying and surrounded by fine lines he hadn't noticed before. He felt a surge of protective care for her and a surge of wild fury at the unknown husband who had frightened her so.

"If you're afraid to tell him, and his friends, that he's not welcome then I'll tell them," Joe said. He got to his feet and stepped back, but not too far. He kept a hand on her shoulder. Even under the towelling robe he could feel the warmth of her skin.

"No, you will *not* say a thing to George or his henchmen." Julia was surprisingly firm. She shook her head.

"It would only provoke them. I'll say whatever has to be said. I just have to work out what that should be."

She frowned, concentrating. Joe waited silently. After a few minutes, Julia clicked her fingers in the air.

"Got it!" she said, excitedly. "I'll tell him the truth! I've rented out the spare room and, naturally, he can't sleep in my bed because I'm divorcing him." Her face was flushed. She avoided looking at Joe. "He can't argue with that, can he?"

Oh, yes he can, Joe thought. He sounds like just the kind of man to argue about another man being in his house. Aloud, he said, "If he's wise he'll stay away, avoid any more trouble with the guards."

"I've thought of a way to make peace with him." Julia left the chair and walked up and down, quickly, agitatedly. "I'll ask him to dinner on Christmas Day. That'll keep him quiet. Sort of. It'll buy some peace, at least." She stopped, a rueful expression on her face. "He's still my husband, technically. And he's Angie's father. It seems to me the least I can do."

Joe didn't argue with her.

He didn't go to work that morning. He left the house all right and, for the benefit of Julia who was waving goodbye from the door, headed in the direction of the library. He called in sick from the first phone box he came to. Then he headed straight for the park. Once there, he sat on a bench for several hours. He didn't notice the cold. He was thinking, considering every angle of the morning's events, working out what was best for him to do.

He was glad he hadn't told Julia the whole truth. He knew she hadn't told him the whole truth of her story either. People were never really honest with one another, in his experience. Not completely honest, anyway. He asked himself too why Julia hadn't called the guards to remove her unwelcome visitors of the night before. The only answer he could come up with, and which he felt reasonably sure was right, was that Julia didn't want trouble any more than he did. She'd clearly had enough grief and unhappiness to last her a lifetime.

As he had himself.

Christmas Day dawned bright and clear. Joe first woke at about six in the morning, aware of a presence in his room. Through half-open eyes, and with his brain half asleep, he saw his bedroom door close on a retreating, white-clad figure.

Julia had left a silver-wrapped

"present from Santa Claus" at the foot of his bed. He opened it slowly. It was a long time, more than twenty-five years, since Santa, or anyone else, had left a Christmas present at the end of his bed. He came from the sort of family in which there was no place, as his mother liked to put it, "for life's useless frills".

The fine, dark-green wool jumper, in a nest of soft tissue inside the silver wrapping paper, was Italian and expensive. He'd never owned one like it.

He wore it going downstairs three hours later, when a flurry of movement assured him that Julia was up and moving about. Mother and daughter were in the kitchen drinking coffee when he arrived in. Angie, dressed in black, gave him what for her was a bright, seasonal grin.

"Morning, Joseph," she said. "A

very Happy Christmas to you." She raised her coffee mug in salute. "I like the jumper," she added, her grin widening.

"I like it myself," Joe said, looking at Julia. "Santa Claus has good taste."

Julia flashed him the pale version of her smile that he'd grown used to in the weeks since the men's visit.

"He got the colour right anyway," she said. "It suits you. Happy Christmas, Joe."

She was dressed quite drably herself. She was wearing a loose brown shirt over jeans. She still looked lovely, because she could not have looked otherwise, but she lacked the sparkle she used to have.

George Ryan, due at three that afternoon for dinner, had not been at all pleased by Julia's refusal to allow him to stay in the house over

Christmas. Julia had already told Joe how he had bullied and blustered when she'd telephoned him in prison the day before his release. He'd even threatened to arrive anyway.

But Joe, standing with an arm about her shoulder, had made sure her resolve didn't weaken. At his bidding, Julia had also phoned the prison governor, telling him of her wishes. As a result, George Ryan had been told, on the day he left prison, that he could visit his wife by invitation only.

Julia was more frightened than reassured. George Ryan made a bad enemy, she said. He would not take being told what to do, and being forbidden the use of what was still legally his home, lying down. He would take revenge, somehow. They would have to be very careful, she said, to be alert and watchful at all times.

Joe wasn't afraid. Not for himself. His concern for Julia was another matter. There were times when he felt fear on her behalf, and a great rage at George Ryan.

"I left presents under the tree," Joe said shyly. Buying the presents had been both a joy and a trial.

Searching through the shops, just another person in the bustling Christmas throng, had been a joy. Wondering if he'd chosen correctly, having no one to confer with and being afraid to ask snooty sales assistants, had been the trial. He'd bought a long woollen scarf for Angie and for Julia a pair of leather gloves with fur trim. Safe enough presents, when you thought about it.

They loved them.

"Oh, Joe!" Julia gave him a quick hug. "You shouldn't have spent so much of your money."

Angie relaxed enough to give him a kiss on the cheek. "Thanks," she said, wrapping the scarf about her neck. "I'll wear it every day."

They stood by the tree, close to the fire Julia had lit earlier, and had Irish coffees made by Joe. After a while they had breakfast. For the day that was in it, Julia had bought smoked salmon and Angie made scrambled eggs. By midday there was nothing for it but to begin preparing the Christmas dinner.

Chapter 8

Julia, making sure nothing could go wrong, had bought pre-cooked turkey, ham and potatoes. The pudding was from the local bakery. The brandy butter and trifle were from the supermarket. All they had to do was cook the vegetables and lay the table.

But, what with Julia taking time out for several nervous drinks and Angie constantly disappearing upstairs to make phone calls, things weren't quite ready when George Ryan rang the doorbell, early, at ten minutes to three.

Angie answered it immediately. Her

father stepped wordlessly inside and crossed briskly to the kitchen without taking off his coat.

"Very festive, Julia. Very festive indeed." He smiled, without mirth, as he stood with his hands in his pockets and surveyed the table. George Ryan had his daughter's dark colouring. But he wasn't as big as Joe had feared. Best not to underestimate his slight frame though. The prison exercise regime would have made him fit and strong.

Prison couldn't be held responsible for the cold, watchful eyes, thin lips and shark-like smile, however. Those features were all of George Ryan's own making.

"You're looking well, George." Julia was cool. She kept her distance, standing with her back to the cooker. "Perhaps you would hang up your coat? You know where the cloakroom is in the hall."

"I heard you had a house guest." George spoke softly, his eyes on Joe. He made no attempt to remove his coat.

"I'm sure your bully-boys have kept you informed," Julia said. "So you must also be aware that Joe is a paying guest."

"He'll be dining with us?" George Ryan didn't raise his voice. Nor, not even for an instant, did he take his eyes off Joe.

"We'll be having Christmas dinner together, yes." Joe took a step forward and held out his hand. "Joe Brown," he said.

George Ryan ignored him. "Not a family meal then?" he said, looking at Julia with an eyebrow raised. Joe dropped his hand.

"What would you like to drink, Dad?" Angie's voice, from the doorway, broke the mounting tension.

"Get me a glass of whiskey, there's my girl." George Ryan turned sharply away from Joe and went with his daughter, arm about her shoulder, into the living-room.

Julia began putting the meal on the table at four o'clock, by which time George Ryan had had several large glasses of whiskey. A subdued Angie watched him cautiously. She kept out of his way as he paced the kitchen, waiting while Julia put the finishing touches to the meal.

"There now." Julia lit the last of the candles and stepped back. "That's everything. You can all take your places."

"And where might my place be?" George asked. "Would you prefer me to sit at the head or foot of this Christmas charade you've prepared, Julia?"

"Sit wherever you like, George," Julia said, shakily. "The table's round so it's all the same where you put yourself. Let's just get started before the food goes cold." She sat down, quickly, on the chair closest to where she'd been standing.

"After you, Mr Brown." George Ryan was exaggeratedly polite, bowing in Joe's direction. "I wouldn't want to take your place at the table."

Joe, without a word, sat on the chair nearest him. Angie did the same. George Ryan remained standing.

"Help yourselves," Julia said, taking her own advice and beginning to heap turkey slices onto her plate. Joe reached out to fork a piece of ham.

"Not so fast, my friend!" George Ryan moved so quickly that Joe didn't even see the knife until it had pinned the sleeve of his new jumper to the table. Julia screamed.

"There's no man going to feed his face at my table before me." George Ryan leaned across the table and held hard onto the handle attached to the long stiletto blade. He hissed into Joe's face. "Drop the meat, Mr Brown."

"You're tearing the sleeve of my jumper," Joe said.

"So I am!" George Brown affected surprise. "Such a fine garment too. Wouldn't be a present from my wife, by any chance? Noticed it when I came in. She gave me one very like it a few Christmases ago. Dear Julia is not over-burdened with imagination, I'm afraid." Smiling his shark's smile, he twisted the blade, deliberately and slowly, catching more of the sleeve, and made the tear bigger.

"Don't, George. Please don't do this." Julia was crying, an edge of hysteria in her voice. "Joe hasn't done you any harm. It's Christmas, for God's sake …"

"No harm?" George Ryan was suddenly shouting, his voice full of boiling rage. "He's moved into my house. He's living off my money. He's very likely in my wife's bed – and you say he's done me no harm? How do you think the set-up here makes me look in front of my mates? In front of my own daughter?"

When he put his free hand on her shoulder, Angie gave a small scream and jerked herself free. She sat then with her head in her hands, shivering.

"Leave her alone, George." Julia spoke quietly.

"How do you think this situation

makes me feel, Julia?" her husband asked again.

Keeping the knife pinned firmly to Joe's sleeve, he leaned across the table. His face, white with fury, was about a foot from Julia's as he went on. "Did you think at all about how I would feel about this clown being here? Did you?"

With his free hand he thumped on the table, too close to where a candle stood in its long silver holder. With a crash, and an arching flame, it toppled and smashed into Joe's wineglass. The wine, a spreading, dark-red pool filled with shards of broken glass, held everyone's silent, shocked attention.

It had covered a good third of the white tablecloth when Joe, enraged and suddenly maniacally strong, erupted from his chair. He grabbed George Ryan by the neck and held him tightly enough to make the other man give a strangled gasp and turn red. Then he lifted him off his feet and propelled him across the room. Pinning him against the wall, inches from the holly wreath hanging there, Joe hit George Ryan three times, hard. The third time Joe's fist smashed into George Ryan's face, blood sprayed from his broken mouth onto the holly leaves.

"Joe – no! Let him go!" Julia's frantic cry came as she bundled Angie out of the kitchen and into the hallway. "That's ENOUGH, Joe! Stop it!" Her scream, as she stood in the open doorway, carried a real and compelling force. Joe stepped away. George Ryan, propped up by the wall, rubbed a hand across his face before looking dazedly at the bloodied result on his palm.

That might have been it. That might have been all that was needed to end what became an unending tragedy for all concerned. It might have if George Ryan, face beginning to swell and eyes venomous, hadn't turned to snarl at his wife. "You'll pay for this, Julia." He took a step in her direction. "I'll get you if it's the last thing I do –"

The sound made by Joe Brown was animal-like. The speed with which he moved back into the fray was inhuman. By the time George Ryan had raised his hands to defend himself it was too late.

Chapter 9

It took Joe and Julia two hours, working flat out, to clean the kitchen of blood.

It took another eight hours to drive George Ryan's body, wrapped in heavy-duty plastic bags, to an isolated County Clare headland. James Mulberry had spent boyhood summers there. Remembering, Joe Brown decided the wintry Atlantic seas surrounding the area would be the ideal place to dispose of the body.

When he toppled the body over the sheer cliff, it quickly disappeared into the heaving, thunderous grey far below. Joe stood for a few minutes with his head bowed. When it started to rain he climbed back into the car.

"Would you like me to drive?" he asked Julia politely.

"Better not," she said. "You're not covered by the insurance."

They headed back to Dublin, travelling without speaking through the remaining hours of darkness. Julia drove slowly and steadily. No point attracting the attention of the guards with speeding or erratic driving. Christmas Day, with its excess of eating and drinking, meant they had the roads almost to themselves as they passed through sleeping small towns, ghostly villages and the deserted countryside.

Joe made plans in his head as they drove along. He knew Julia must be doing the same thing. It was all about survival now, each man and woman for him or herself. They were on the outskirts of Dublin when he said, "You set me up, didn't you?"

Julia sighed. "You set yourself up," she said.

"You knew all about me when I came to your door that day, didn't you?" Joe said.

"I knew who you were," Julia agreed.

"Your ad in the Spar was meant for me, wasn't it?" Joe didn't wait for an answer. "You read the newspaper reports of the court case long before you met me." Joe watched her, not expecting an answer. She half smiled but didn't turn. "You probably did some private investigating as well. You had the contacts. The lag who put me onto the hostel was one. Easy enough, too, to make life unpleasant for me once I got there."

"I talked to a few people, yes." Julia spoke at last. "I thought we could be of use to one another –"

"The room was the bait," Joe interrupted harshly. "It was a way of trapping me into your plan to be rid of your husband and have his money for yourself ..." He paused. "It was perfect, Julia. A perfect plan and perfectly done. You're rid of George Ryan and the money's all yours." He turned to her. "But what now?"

"Not so perfect a plan, Joe." Julia's face was pale and hard as stone. "I thought you would beat George up, nothing more. Frighten him into leaving me alone." She shook her head. Her voice, when she went on, was bleak. "I knew your reputation, that you could fly into a murderously jealous rage when provoked. I saw something in your face in the newspaper pictures …"

"You saw James Mulberry in my face," Joe said. "You saw the part of me that's given to senseless rage, the madness in me that had already driven me to kill a man because of a woman. The bit of me I thought I'd got rid of when I became Joe Brown."

"Something like that," Julia agreed.

"You watched me come and go to the Spar for a while, I suppose?" Joe said.

"I had Angie watch you. I didn't want you to see and remember me."

"All you had to do was get me on side." Joe shrugged. "Your side. You knew your husband would create a scene and that I'd lose it. The jumper was just to make sure, wasn't it?"

"Yes." She turned to look at him,

briefly. Her expression seemed sincerely regretful.

"Only, I just wanted you to hurt him. Nothing more."

"You would have kept me on in the house, of course," Joe said bitterly. "Your pet bully-boy. A sort of in-house bodyguard."

"That's an unpleasant way of putting it."

"It's the truth of things," Joe said harshly. "I would have been tied to you then. You'd have made sure of that, allowing me all the comforts of home and friendship as long as I paid the price. Always with the threat that you might expose me."

"All that's changed now, anyway," Julia said. She turned the car up along the Grand Canal. They were only minutes from the house. "I'll have to go away now. So will you. It being

Christmas will make it easy enough to slip out of the country. I'll give you the money to go too. We'll get tickets at the airport this evening. You go your way, Joe, and Angie and I will go ours. The guards can't do anything until they find his body. And that'll take months – if they ever do find it. We'll be well hidden by then, Angie and I. We'll have a new life. So will you, if you've any sense."

"You're not afraid of me?" Joe said.

"No. I'm not afraid of you."

She was right not to be afraid of him. He wasn't a murderer – not him, not Joe Brown. He was someone with an unfortunate other side, someone who flipped, lost to a crazy, jealous anger in certain situations. He would just have to avoid such situations in the future.

The last time Joe saw Julia Ryan she

was crossing the tarmac to the plane waiting to take herself and Angie to Amsterdam. The taller of the two men who'd called that night in December was by her side, his arm about her shoulders. She was looking up at him, laughing into his face. It wasn't until then that he knew, at last and for sure, that she had lied. She had set him up to kill George Ryan.

Joe Brown would find her. Whatever it took, and wherever she went, he would find her. And he would kill her. She'd been wrong to trust him. He would kill her if it was the last thing he did.

OPEN DOOR SERIES

TRADE/CREDIT CARD ORDERS TO:
CMD, 55A Spruce Avenue,
Stillorgan Industrial Park,
Blackrock, Co. Dublin, Ireland.
Tel: (+353 1) 294 2560
Fax: (+353 1) 294 2564

TO PLACE PERSONAL/EDUCATIONAL
ORDERS OR TO ORDER A CATALOGUE
PLEASE CONTACT:
New Island, 2 Brookside, Dundrum
Road, Dundrum,
Dublin 14, Ireland.
Tel: (+353 1) 298 6867/298 3411
Fax: (+353 1) 298 7912
www.newisland.ie